In the same series:

THE CITY OF FLOWERS
Constance Savery

RUNAWAY JACK
Christine Wood

THE NEW BRIDGE
Elisabeth Batt

HIDEAWAY HOUSE

STELLA LILLIAN

LUTTERWORTH PRESS · LONDON

ISBN 0 7188 1881 4

*Printed in Great Britain by
Richard Clay (The Chaucer Press), Ltd.,
Bungay, Suffolk*

CONTENTS

CHAPTER ONE

WALKING FOR OXFAM

"I WISH," said Lucy, her eyes on the long road stretching before her, "I'd never come."

She had a great big blister on her heel and her shoe was rubbing it raw. She was hot and tired. The hill up which they trudged grew steeper with every step. In the wooded valley there had been deep shade from the heat of this July day, but that was gone now. They were out in the open country again.

Emma, ahead of Lucy, taking great strides with her long legs, swung round. "You should have soaped your feet," she said. "I told you to."

"You're always telling me things," Lucy said.

"And what's the use when you don't listen?"

"I do listen."

"Then why couldn't you do as I said?"

"I never meant to come—that's why," said Lucy, limping, trying to keep up. "It was you, Emma Knight, that got me in on this walking for Oxfam. You persuaded me. It's *your* fault. And what my father's going to say if he finds out——"

"You mean—you didn't *tell* him?"

"Of course I didn't. He would have said no."

Emma whistled, and went striding on. "And him so goody!" she exclaimed. "Saying no to a cause like Oxfam! Does your father ever say yes? I know you've been ill, but you're better now. If he would have said no, and you didn't want to come, why did you let me persuade you?"

Feeling tears begin to prick, Lucy gave a quick sniff. "I wanted to help." A tear was beginning to slide down her cheek. She dashed it away—before Emma saw it.

"You thought of all the money you'd make," said Emma in exultant tones. "I'm going to make lots. Think of the money and forget your heel."

"I *can't* forget it," Lucy wailed. "And *look*——" stopping, she twisted round, "there's another blister coming on the other heel now! Emma . . . I can't go much farther."

"You can't *give up*," Emma cried. "Not *yet*. We've done no more than ten miles!"

"It *hurts*, Emma."

"I suppose it does," said Emma in a pitying voice. "Oh, *Lucy*, you poor little thing."

For the next six steps Lucy didn't answer. She couldn't. She was much too busy choking back the tears. Every step was pure pain. And she didn't like being called "a little thing". Not everyone could grow as big and tall as Emma. Besides, Emma was older. She was eleven.

"If I'm slow," said Lucy, "you're unkind."

"I'm not unkind," Emma cried. "I'd buy you a new pair of feet—if I could," and she put her arm round Lucy, to help her along. And that made everything worse. Being forced to go faster it hurt far more.

"Do you think," said Lucy, with a sob in her voice she couldn't suppress, "they'll laugh at me, think me—soft . . . if I give up?"

"But all those people who have sponsored you— what will *they* think?"

"I don't care. I can't go on. Emma . . ." Lucy drew a deep breath, "do you know what?"

"Of course I know what! We're coming to it. It's round this bend—half hidden in the trees. Bessley Manor!" and Emma gave a little skip.

"I dream about it," Lucy said.

"Me, too," said Emma, "but not at night. Only in the day. I make up stories."

"I wonder if yours are the same as mine?"

"Of course they aren't. They couldn't be."

"Emma—you're going too fast. Emma . . ."

"Well?"

"If they're not locked, I'm going to open the manor gates and—go in."

"Go in!" Emma's eyes widened. "You *can't*, Lucy. You know what it says. TRESPASSERS WILL BE PROSECUTED."

"I know, but—I've got to go *somewhere*, haven't I? I've got to get out of this! And . . . I want to walk among those trees, and I want to see inside the house. I've always wanted."

"You're not the only one. I want too. We both want to see inside the house. And I believe, Lucy Winter, you're just pretending you've got sore heels—so you can go and look through the windows. You're mean. And I'll tell the man——"

"What man?"

"Him," said Emma, tossing a glance over her shoulder. "The man in the car."

"Oh," said Lucy, "*him*. It's you, Emma, that's mean. You know I'm not pretending."

"What if I do? You're not to go without *me*."

Lucy didn't answer that. "Look," she said

wonderingly, as rounding a bend at the top of the hill they glimpsed the roof of the old mansion, "there it it. It's not been painted for fifty years. It looks like a house nobody loves."

"I love it," said Emma. "It's a horrid shame!"

"I love it, too. There's a lake in the garden," Lucy said, "I could bathe my feet!"

"No," said Emma, "you *can't* bathe your feet. Not alone. It might not be safe. It might not be— empty. The house, I mean."

"It *is* empty."

"Somebody might be hiding there. A tramp. A whole gang of tramps. They'd set on you. Chase you away. And if you can't walk with blisters on your heels you wouldn't be able to run!"

"All I want to do," said Lucy with a sigh, "is to sit down."

And it was just at that moment that the man in the car, who had been following them for the last two miles, drew level.

"Trouble?" he asked.

He had a twinkle in his green-grey eyes. Lucy knew him at once as "the man with the orange tree". That was a shock. She didn't know his name, but he lived in the house where the greenhouses were at the end of their avenue! Suppose he recognized her? Suppose her father got to know?

"Tired?" he asked.

"Blisters," said Emma. "Not me, of course. I soaped my heels. I told Lucy, but," Emma shook her head, "Lucy doesn't hear."

He looked surprised. "You mean—she's deaf?"

"Not really," said Emma, beginning to giggle.

"Ah," he said, "I see what you mean," and he laughed too. It was lovely laughter. Or so Lucy thought. Not like Emma's, going up and up. Just a deep chuckle. In spite of her worry Lucy found herself smiling as well, and when he turned to open the rear door, she climbed in, thankfully, without a word.

"How many miles," Emma asked, "has Lucy done?"

"Eleven," he said, as the car moved on again.

"I'm going to finish," Emma declared, and off she set, swinging her handbag as she went.

Lucy felt shy. And ashamed. "I couldn't help it," she said. "My heels are so sore."

"Of course you can't help it," he replied. "Your friend is used to walking and you are not."

"How do you know?" she asked. Oh, bother! She hoped he didn't know who she was.

Busy turning the corner, he made no reply. But he was kind. He was excusing her, and that made her feel better. For Emma *was* used to walking. She went with her father and mother for long tramps. Or she used to. They didn't go now, Emma said.

She watched him. He was about thirty-three, she thought, like her Dad. But her Dad was beginning to go bald, and this man wasn't. His hair was thick and dark and curly. He was driving the car slowly and carefully, watching out for more casualties. But the silence worried Lucy. She liked to talk. She wondered what she could talk about? He liked gardening, she knew that. He had more garden than anyone else because his was the end house and the

corner took a wide sweep, so there was plenty of
room for those great big hothouses. He grew orchids.
And he had a banana plant. And an orange tree.
She was just thinking that perhaps he would like to
talk about his plants when he said: "I know your
father. That's why I know you're not used to
walking. And you've been ill."

Bother! Lucy smothered a great gasp, but he must
have heard. That knocked all thought of making
conversation right out of her head.

"You're Lucy Winter and you live in the house
called Pear Trees in Friar's Avenue."

What could she do now? "I really shouldn't be
here," she said, her voice small. "If my father
finds out he'll be cross."

"Because you've been ill?"

"Yes," said Lucy, "but I'm better now. He
doesn't understand. I *have* to do things. It makes me
feel silly to keep saying no. So, Mr——"

"Craig," he said. "Jeremy Craig."

"So, Mr. Craig, you won't tell him, will you—that
—we met?"

He took so long to answer Lucy began to bite her
lip. She always did that when she was anxious.

"I could forget it, I suppose."

"Oh, yes, please. You see, Daddy worries. And
it's such a nuisance. It stops me doing all the things I
want to do. I can't draw and paint all day—oh,
Emma's disappeared!"

"She's just turned the corner. A fine walker, that
girl."

"Yes," said Lucy. "Do you know her?"

"No, who is she? Tell me about her."

"Oh . . . well . . . she lives in Maple Road and she's nice! She's just as nice as her legs are long! We met in the park, and that's where we always meet. She has two brothers, but most of the time they're at boarding school and I don't know them. I don't know Mrs. Knight either, or Mr Knight. I don't think they're happy together. Mr. and Mrs. I mean. It worries Emma. It makes her cry. It is a worry, isn't it, when your parents don't get on?"

Mr. Craig shook his head. "I've no knowledge of that, I'm afraid."

"You mean—it didn't happen to you? It didn't happen to me, either. But you can imagine it, can't you?"

"Perhaps I can."

"Oh, I can. I know *exactly* how Emma feels. You see . . . my mother died last year—and I know how I should feel if Mummy and Daddy had fought. It would have been—*dreadful*. I don't know *what* I should have done. It spoils Emma's life, you know. Makes her miserable."

"I hadn't thought of that."

"How could you when you didn't know her? Oh—I wish I'd done better," Lucy sighed.

"Now don't you worry. You did your best."

Lucy shook her head. "That wasn't my best."

CHAPTER TWO

FOUND OUT

It was so comfortable sitting in the car Lucy had almost forgotten her heels were sore. She'd been happy too, talking to Mr. Craig. She liked him enormously. On the way home she said to Emma: "When I grow up I'm going to marry a man just like Mr. Craig."

"Like *him*?" Emma's eyes widened. "But he's so old. And what about Timothy Pearce?"

"I've changed my mind. You can have Tim."

"I don't want to get married at all," said Emma.

"Why ever not?"

They were standing at the park gates. Friar's Avenue was just round the corner and Maple Road lay the other way. Picking at the mortar in a small crevice Emma said: "I would ... if I could be sure he'd really love me. Love me for ever. But you can't be sure."

"You can," said Lucy. "I know you can. My Mum and Dad were terribly in love. They were—well—like one person. But then—they'd found the secret, and it was *that* that made them happy."

"The secret?"

"Yes," said Lucy, smiling to herself. "It's a lovely secret. But they wouldn't mind me telling you—if you'd like me to tell you."

"Of course I'd like you to tell me."

"Well," Lucy's voice sank to a whisper, "they were married to Jesus—as well as to each other.

They still are, even though Mummy's in Heaven and Daddy's on earth. I don't *quite* understand, but Daddy says I will when I'm older. It made them—terribly happy."

"Then I wish my Mum and Dad would jolly well find that secret!" cried Emma in a loud voice. "I wish they'd get married to Jesus Christ! Can anybody do it? Or do you have to be special?"

"Of course you don't have to be special! But you have to believe in Jesus Christ—believe He's the Son of God. You know about Jesus?"

"He was crucified. But I don't know why."

"You don't know *why*? What do they teach you at *your* school?"

"Not much," said Emma. "What good did it do—being crucified?"

"Goodness me! Don't you know? He died to save us from our sins. He died instead of us. He died, and rose again! So God forgives us now when we do wrong, for Jesus' sake. I knew this years ago—when I was a *baby*," Lucy said with satisfaction.

"Well," said Emma, "I jolly well didn't! Go on."

"Jesus Christ conquered death—there, on that cross. Didn't you *know*?"

"No," said Emma, picking at the mortar.

"Fancy you not knowing that. The Lord Jesus Christ has eternal life and He wants to give it to us. He wants us to live with Him for ever. We're able to have this eternal life, but we're all dead—like an electric kettle, or a fire, until we're made one with the 'power', with the 'life' that Jesus has. He has the power to make us come alive, but we can't come alive

until we're made one with Him. Do you see, Emma?
That's how Daddy explained it to me. Like plugging
in to the power in the wall."

"I see *that*."

"I don't *quite* understand myself, but our sins,
Daddy says, are like dirty connections. We have to
be all cleaned up and forgiven, then the Lord Jesus
Christ can give us His life. And He can give us His
strength, too, when we feel all unhappy and frightened and we don't know what in the world to do.
Like—when Mummy died."

Emma was silent. Then she said: "I think it's my
Mum."

"Your Mum? Your Mum's pretty, you said."

"Of course she's pretty. Like your Mum was. But
my Mum's tall and—well—I know you loved your
Mum terribly, but my Mum's the loveliest person
you ever saw."

"Is she?" said Lucy wonderingly. "And your
Dad? What's he like?"

"He's wonderful too. All brown and—he's always
looking at the clouds! And that's a bother. He's an
artist, you see. That's why. He likes painting clouds.
All his spare time——"

"Emma! You never told me your father was an
artist! You mean he *paints*?"

"Of course he paints."

Lucy took a deep breath. "I wish my Dad
did."

"Don't you go wishing any such thing! It's a
nuisance—it gets in the way——"

"But I *do* wish, Emma. I——"

"Oh, yes, I know," cried Emma. "You want to

paint trees. You're always wanting to paint *trees*. I think it's a bore."

"It's better than walking," Lucy retorted. "You don't get all hot and covered with blisters! It makes you feel—all bubbly inside."

"I don't see why. It's not ginger pop."

"Well, it does." Lucy swung away. "I'm going now. I hope Dad won't notice I'm limping."

But he did.

Lucy was on the sofa with her legs tucked under her, reading, when he came in, and she thought she was safe, until he said, "You look tired, Lucy. Were you painting today?"

"No," she said; then, "Yes." Then she blushed. She'd told a lie.

"Show me," he said. "What did you paint?"

"But——I left it upstairs."

"Then run up and get it."

"But——"

"You said, Lucy, you weren't tired."

"I'm not, but——"

"Fetch it," he said, "I'd like to see it," and he looked so tired himself Lucy didn't know what to do. She wanted to hug him, to throw her arms around his neck and cry: Daddy, Daddy, don't look so sad. But instead she jumped to her feet and made for the door, to fetch a painting she hadn't done that day, and somehow that lie she'd told made her throat feel thick. Because it wasn't easy to lie to Daddy when he was tired and sad; and she was standing by the door trying to swallow that lie, to get rid of the taste, when he said, "Lucy."

B

"Yes, Daddy."

"What's the matter with your heels?"

She took a deep breath. She couldn't tell a lie again. "I've—been walking for Oxfam."

"Walking for Oxfam? How far?"

"Not far, Daddy. Not very far. Just—as far as the the house."

"The house? Oh, you mean the old manor?"

Lucy nodded. "Yes. Then a man picked me up in his car. He was kind. He lives where the big green-houses are—at the end of the avenue. He knows you, Daddy."

"Craig, you mean. Well . . . I'm glad you told me the truth, Lucy. Did you enjoy it?"

Lucy stared. "Enjoy it? Telling the truth?"

Her father smiled. "What I meant was, did you enjoy the walk?"

"No, I *hated* it. And I'm sorry, Daddy. I wish now I'd asked you, and I wish you had said: Certainly not! It was Emma's fault. She persuaded me. She made me feel mean."

"Emma? Who's Emma?"

"My friend. We met in the park. Her Dad's an artist. Not all the time. For fun, you know."

Her father said, "You mean John Knight?"

"Oh—do you know him? His name is Knight. I don't know his Christian name, but then—he isn't a Christian. So he can't have one."

"Lucy! You must *not* pass judgement."

"But Emma *said* he wasn't! And she knows."

"And what about Emma? Is she a Christian?"

"Oh, no," said Lucy, "she's not a Christian either. They are none of them Christians. Emma thinks I'm quaint when I talk about God. But that doesn't stop me talking! Because God's wonderful and it would be terribly lonely without Him. What would *you* do, Daddy, without God? You'd still be crying for Mummy, wouldn't you? But you've stopped crying now, like me, because you know she's safe, and you're thinking of all that glory, and how pretty she'll look in the dazzling light. I wish we could see her."

"I wish so too, my sweet."

"And you don't really mind about my heels?"

"Of course I mind."

"But you're not *cross*, I mean?"

"How *can* I be cross?" Her father sighed, held out his hand to her, and drawing her down on to his knee he stroked her hair, the long dark hair so like her mother's. "You wanted to be kind, my sweet. I know you did. As long as you don't overtax your strength, my precious. Have you made a lot of money for the starving people?" and he looked at her inquiringly.

"Ye-es," said Lucy, "but I wish I'd made more. A lot of people sponsored me."

"I'm sure they did. And you never asked *me*."

Lucy blushed, and bit her lip.

"Suppose, my sweet, I give you—how much a mile? Five pence?"

She blushed deeper. "Thank you," she whispered.

CHAPTER THREE

"WHAT'S THE MATTER?"

The following morning Emma rang up. "I'll meet you in the park," she said, "in just ten minutes."

"What for?" asked Lucy.

"To collect our sponsor money, of course. Have you counted up, Lucy, how much you'll get?"

"Not quite," Lucy said, though she knew almost to the last five pence piece.

"You'll be jealous when you know how much I've made!"

"I won't," said Lucy, but she knew she would. She didn't like being beaten. And she couldn't help being envious though she knew it was wrong. Worse than that—the thought of having to ring all those doorbells to ask for the money, and then to have to admit that she'd walked no more than eleven miles. That made her feel small.

She had meant to walk twenty—like Emma. Then she would have carried her head high—as Emma could. Watching her mother's friends she would have felt sure they were thinking: What a splendid girl she is. And now they would think: She didn't do much, did she? They would think her a "poor little thing"—as Emma had said.

It was then the thought sprang up in her mind! And there she was—listening to it with her inward ears, and listening to Emma with her outward ones.

And when Emma said: "I'm not going to tell

you until we get to the park," Lucy said: "All right. See you——" and put down the receiver.

She had to ring off because the thought was growing so fast there was no room in her mind for anything else. In fact, it had grown so big and strong it had almost ceased to be just a thought. It was ready to become an action.

She ran from the house. One of the best things, she felt, about the summer holidays was the flowers in the park. There were hundreds and hundreds, splashing their bright colours everywhere—yellow, orange, pink, red. The sun had broken through now. But the wind was cool.

"Twenty sponsors!" Emma exclaimed, waving her paper when Lucy appeared, "and they're all for five pence a mile!"

"All?" asked Lucy.

"I wouldn't take less. You can't offer less than that for a cause like Oxfam! Can you?"

"Some of mine," Lucy answered, "are for only three pence."

"You shouldn't take it," Emma declared. "Think of the blisters!"

Lucy *was* thinking of them. She couldn't forget them. But it was too late now to double her earnings. Besides, her sponsors were not as well off as Emma's, and that made a difference.

"How much will you make?" she asked in a small voice.

"Twenty pounds!" cried Emma in delight.

"Oh . . ." Lucy turned to look at Emma envyingly. And then the envy died. There was something queer about Emma today. One moment she was all aglow, rejoicing over that twenty pounds, and the next she was like a dead stick. All the life gone out of her. She just sat staring at the flowers. But Lucy felt she was not looking at them at all; she was thinking of something quite different.

She had to know what was making Emma so still and silent. "What's the matter, Emma?"

Emma didn't answer. Instead she picked up a stone and flung it into the flower bed!

"Emma! What *is* the matter?"

"I wish I knew! But—I *do* know. They've *quarrelled*. About a man. I heard them. Lucy . . . I think they're sending me to boarding school."

"The same as your brothers."

"But I'm *not* the same as my brothers! I'm *not*, Lucy. I live at home——I must——I——"

"Wouldn't you like," asked Lucy in a wondering voice, "to go to boarding school?" It was something she had always wanted to try.

"*No*, I would *not*. And they wouldn't send me if they were happy! They want me out of the way, that's why. Something *terrible* is going to happen. I can feel it—here—in my chest," and Emma gave herself a big thump.

"You mean——"

"Yes, I *do* mean. There's a man, Lucy. I know there is. Mummy—Daddy—they'll get a divorce. And, Lucy . . ." Emma's voice broke, "I can't *bear* it. They'll send me off to boarding school and when I come back . . . there'll be no home." The tears began rolling down Emma's cheeks. "We'll be torn in bits—Mummy, Daddy, the boys, and me. What shall I do,"—sniffing and gulping Emma went on,—"what

shall I do, Lucy, what shall I do? You must help me
. . . help me. *Do* something, Lucy."

Emma was always the same. Let something go
wrong and someone must wave a magic wand
and get her out of her troubles the very next minute.
But this—what could Emma expect her, Lucy,
to do about a problem like this? "What *can* I do?"
Lucy exclaimed. "I don't even *know* your father
and mother. And if I did—they wouldn't listen
to *me*."

"They might," said Emma, her mouth twisting.

"Emma, they wouldn't. Please don't cry."

"I *want* to cry. It's all here in my chest and it's
making me—sick. It's all right for you, saying don't
cry, but you would if—"

"Yes, I would. I'm sorry. Really I am."

"If you were *really* sorry," Emma said, sniffing
back the tears and chewing her handkerchief, "you'd
help me to do something."

"But, Emma, . . . I don't know what to do!"

"Then you *should* know! You're always talking
about God and what *He* can do. If He's the sort of
person you say He wouldn't let things like this
happen. He wouldn't *allow* people to be made unhappy. Why *doesn't* He stop it?"

"How do *I* know why He doesn't stop it! But He
could," said Lucy fiercely, "if He thought that was
the right thing to do! I know He could. But I
don't suppose he was—well, consulted."

"*Consulted?*"

"Yes. You know what that means—don't you?"

"Of course I know! Why should He be consulted?
If you think my father and mother are going to

go asking God what they should do, you've got it all wrong, Lucy Winter."

"That's what I said, didn't I? He wasn't consulted. They didn't *ask* for His help."

"Does He have to be *asked*?"

"Of course He does. God has very good manners. He doesn't push His nose where it isn't wanted."

"I call that silly," Emma exclaimed. "Why can't He *make* my Mum and Dad stop quarrelling?"

"Stupid! God doesn't *make* people do anything. And I'm glad He doesn't! Think how awful it would be."

"I know," said Emma, "what I shall do! When I've collected my money—I shall run away!"

"You mean—go to your Aunt Veronica?"

"Of course I don't mean Aunt Veronica! They'd find me there. Besides, she'd tell."

"Then where will you go?"

Emma sniffed; then blew her nose in a businesslike manner. "Yes—that's what I'll do. I'll run away. And . . ." her face brightened, "they'll be so upset they won't quarrel any more!"

"Oh . . ." said Lucy. "Well . . . perhaps they won't." They'd be terribly upset, she was sure of that. So it might be a good idea. The thought of what her father's feelings would be if *she* ran away made Lucy gasp.

"Emma—do you think you should?"

"Of course I should!"

"Emma, where will you go?

"I know where I'll go."

"*Where?* Where, Emma?"

"Where I've always wanted to go—and on my

own—without grown-ups, I mean. And now I shall. And Lucy, you mustn't tell."

"I don't tell."

"They might try to make you."

"They can't, stupid! Your father and mother don't even know we're friends."

"So they don't! I'd forgotten that. Isn't that lucky?" Emma laughed. "Let's collect the money," she said, and up she jumped.

"You don't mean," said Lucy slowly, "you're going to use the money to run away?"

"Of course I'm not going to use it to run away. That would be stealing."

"Yes . . ." said Lucy, and the thought that was still in her mind shrank from that word stealing and made her uncomfortable.

"Lucy," said Emma, standing by the seat, drawing on the path with her toe, "do you think they'll be *very* upset?"

"How do I know?" Lucy answered, her mind so full of the thought that she couldn't give Emma her full attention.

"Well, *your* father, would *he* be upset if *you* ran away?"

"He'd be downright frantic," Lucy replied, her mind swinging back to Emma's problem. "It's a wicked thing to do."

"You're always saying things are wicked! But I tell you, Lucy, I *know* what's going to happen. And if I'm good—and do nothing—it *will* happen. I've got to *stop* it."

"By being wicked?" Lucy frowned. She thought she knew the difference between right and wrong,

but now . . . she was all mixed up. Was it right for
Emma to run away because she thought her parents
would be so distressed they'd turn to one another
again, or was it wrong? She understood how Emma
felt—she would feel exactly the same, yet——

"I don't care, Lucy Winter, what you think! If
I'm being wicked, *they're* being wicked. If *I'm* not
kind *they're* not kind either! They'll send me off to
boarding school and——"

"Boarding school," said Lucy hopefully, "might
be wonderful fun." She felt she ought to try to find
some line of argument to stop Emma running away.
It was such a dreadful thing to do. Besides, she
would miss her. And she was afraid. There were
visions in her mind already of policemen with dogs
out looking for Emma, just as she'd seen them on
television. "There'll be a terrible fuss if you run
away."

"Well, I'm going to. But I haven't much money—
of my own, I mean——" and Emma paused.

Lucy didn't answer.

"I haven't much money," Emma said again when
she found only silence. "I wonder how much money
you've got, Lucy?"

"I've got five pence."

"You don't mean to say you've spent that eighty-
five pence you had last week?"

"I bought Daddy a tie and a birthday card."

"You mean it was your Dad's birthday! Oh . . ."

"You can have the five pence if you like."

"What use will *that* be!"

"If you don't want it," Lucy replied, "I can spend
it myself."

"Couldn't you ask your Dad for more?"

"No, I couldn't! And I won't! It would be like asking him to pay for his own present!"

"So it would," and Emma fell silent. Then she said in a loud voice: "If *I* believed in God and *my* friend needed a few odd pence I'd ask Him, and I'd expect Him to give them to me."

"All right," said Lucy with a quick gasp— "all right, Emma, I *will*! But I must go home to ask Him. I must—kneel down."

Emma shrugged. "Just as you like," she said. "I'm off to collect my money."

Lucy flew home. Into the house she rushed, up the stairs—to fling herself down beside her bed covered with a rose-pink spread.

And then, she didn't know what to say.

Usually the words came tumbling out, but now as she knelt there she felt as though she were starched. Quite stiff. The words wouldn't come. "Please God," she began.

She tried again. "Please, Lord Jesus——"

She had come home to ask for money for Emma and ask she would—if she had to *drag* the words out of herself. "Please, God, help me to get some money so Emma can run away——"

She stopped. God might not like a prayer like that! You had to ask for good things, or you wouldn't get them. And she was not at all sure that it was a good thing for Emma to run away——in fact, she was sure it wasn't. God would never approve of Emma making her parents anxious, so He wouldn't be willing to help her to do it. And yet . . . if she

could just ask somebody what they should do, but
that would mean telling. And she had promised
Emma she wouldn't tell.

Kneeling there, thinking, chewing her thumb,
Lucy saw one thing clearly. Emma trusted her. And
when your friend trusted you, you had to stand by
her. And poor Emma . . . she didn't know anything
much about God. And when you knew nothing about
Him and you were in trouble you were terribly lonely.
Because God was your help. Her mother had said so.
Her Dad said the same. They had *proved* it, they
said. So it must be true.

The difficulty was, He seemed so far away. Out of
reach. She needed His help; she wanted to ask Him
what to do, and she didn't know how to get to Him.
You knelt down, of course, as she was doing now.
And you told him all the trouble, even when the
words got stuck and wouldn't come out. But . . . it
was like talking to the bed!

"Emma's unhappy," she cried. "She's *unhappy*.
Help me, Lord—help me to get some money so
Emma can run away."

And she felt as though the pink bedspread stuffed
the words right back into her mouth! She swallowed,
got up quickly, and ran back to the park.

CHAPTER FOUR

A WRONG THING TO DO

EMMA had gone, of course. Sitting on the seat once more, Lucy took out her sponsor card and added again (she'd added it five times already) how much money she could claim.

Compared with Emma's twenty pounds, it looked very little. She had eight sponsors, four for five pence a mile, and four for three pence. And she had walked eleven miles.

Right then the thought darted back into her mind. Why not say she had walked fifteen? That would solve all her problems. She wouldn't be a bit ashamed to say she had walked fifteen. And she would get some money for Emma.

Yet she wasn't sure she ought to do it. Her thoughts had a battle. One kept saying it was a wrong thing to do. It was stealing, as Emma had said. But another said it was quite all right. She didn't want the money for herself. She wanted it to help Emma. Emma *needed* the money. How could adding on a few miles matter when the cause was good? Nobody'd miss a few pence more.

No, nobody would. Jumping up, she went off to the first house where Mrs. Robinson, she thought, eyed her somewhat doubtfully.

"And did you really walk fifteen miles when you've been so poorly? I wonder your father allowed it," she said. "You did do well," and she counted out the money and put it in Lucy's hand.

"There," she said, "you deserve a clap!"

"Thank you," said Lucy, beaming with pleasure. She went down the road then, to Mrs. Murdock.

Mrs. Murdock patted her shoulder. "You're a *fine girl*. Growing up pretty. Them eyes of yours. I was saying only last night—that Lucy Winter, she's not got the good looks now maybe, but them eyes of hers, they'll do something for her when she's older. How far did you say—fifteen miles? Good for you. I'm pleased to help."

Lucy smiled. When she got home she must look in the glass and see what her eyes were really like. Now for Mrs. Tomlinson.

When she had all the money collected, she had to divide the honest money from the other. She had one pound and twenty-eight pence to give to Emma. She had managed all right without God after all. And then a terrible thought came into her mind. *Suppose Emma wouldn't take it?*

Why hadn't she thought of that before? She knew what Emma had said—"That would be stealing"—and here she was with stolen money for Emma.

To count the money and divide it she had gone back to the park, and now, as she slipped it back into her bag, she felt her face grow redder and redder. She didn't see Emma come in through the gate— running. Lucy never knew Emma was there until Emma sat down on the seat beside her and said: "Have you got it all collected?"

Lucy couldn't look up. Emma gave her a dig with her elbow and said: "Are you asleep?"

"No . . ." said Lucy. "I wish I were."

"What's happened?" cried Emma. "Your money
—didn't you get it? Did they all turn crusty?"

"No," said Lucy in a voice that squeaked.

'Then what's the matter?"

"Emma—I got some money for you, but——"

"Lucy, you're *super!* You mean you prayed to
your God and He gave you what you asked
for?"

"No ... I asked Him, but——"

"What did He say?"

'I don't know."

"Then what's the use! You might just as well
talk to the birds!"

"*No!*" said Lucy, almost shouting.

She couldn't have Emma saying things like that!
And she thought about that bedspread stuffing the
words back into her mouth. Or *was* it the bedspread?
Perhaps it was—she didn't know——

"Emma," she cried, "there was something wrong
with my prayer. It ... wouldn't rise."

"*Rise?*" said Emma, her eyes wide. "You mean—
it wouldn't go up? Does it have to go up?"

Lucy didn't know, because—well—God was so
close, He could hear the slightest whisper. In fact
He was so close you didn't need to whisper at all.
He knew what you were thinking and feeling. All
the same——

"There was something wrong with it, Emma, and
—it was pushed back into my mouth."

"Pushed back into your mouth!" Emma's eyes
grew wider still. "Who pushed it?"

"I tell you—there was something wrong with it.
So ... it went back where it came from."

"Oh . . ." said Emma, her eyes round with thought. "What was wrong with it?"

"It wasn't a right prayer. And God won't have anything to do with wrong prayers. He can't."

"Why wasn't it right?"

"I'm not sure, but . . . you see I was asking for money so you could run away, and that's wrong. Your father and mother—they'd be worried to death. They'd call in the police——"

"I'm going anyway! How much money have you got for me? Lucy . . . how did you get the money?"

Lucy looked away. "I wish I hadn't got it."

Emma stared. "You don't mean you—*stole* it?"

"I did it for you."

"Goodness gracious, Lucy! I didn't mean you to steal it! What did you do?"

"I said I walked fifteen miles."

"*Lucy Winter!*"

"Emma! I did it for *you*."

"Well, I don't want you to do things like that for me!" Lucy saw Emma's eyes flash. She looked so cross Lucy was afraid. "*I* didn't ask you to lie and steal. I asked you to ask your God, that's all, and if *that's* what He told you——"

"He didn't, Emma, He didn't! He would never, *never* tell anyone to do what I did." Lucy was shaken by a great sob. "I've told you, I didn't pray the right prayer, and I haven't done the right thing, but—Emma, I *did* do it for *you*. I wanted to help. Please believe me."

"I don't know that I do. One thing I know—you didn't like being beaten. You didn't like telling people you'd only walked eleven miles. You did it,

Lucy Winter, because you want people to think you are smarter than you are!"

"I did it for you, too."

"You did it for yourself. You lied, and you stole. I wonder what your God thinks about that?"

Lucy gave a great sigh. "I'm wondering too."

"You'd better ask Him, Lucy Winter. But Lucy . . . if you told your God I wanted help—would that be a right prayer?"

Lucy gulped. "Yes, I think it would."

"Do it then."

"What—here in the park?"

"Does it matter where you do it?"

"No . . . I don't think it does. But—Emma— what *sort* of help are you asking for?"

Emma twitched her shoulders in exasperation. "If your God is alive and real I want Him to help my father and mother to love one another, to be happy together. Is that too hard for Him?"

"Of course not! Nothing is too hard for God."

"Well, then. I don't care how He does it. I just want help. So, ask."

"Why don't *you* ask?"

"I don't know Him, stupid. He's not *my* friend. He's *yours*. You can't go asking people to do things for you when you don't *know* them."

Lucy sat silent. Her friend He might be, but she didn't feel she knew Him either. Not really. She merely knew *about* Him, from listening to what her father and mother said. Her father knew Him, she felt sure of that. And her mother must have known Him well. God had been their friend for such a long time that they liked to spend time in His company,

c

just to be with Him, without, sometimes, saying a word. Like you do with someone you love very much.

"I don't know Him either," said Lucy in a small voice. "I'm just learning about Him, getting to know Him. But He likes children."

"Then ask, Lucy. *Do* something."

"Be quiet then. He won't expect me to kneel with all these people around. I'll whisper it."

Waiting in silence, Emma watched, and when Lucy opened her eyes she asked: "Did it go up?"

Lucy nodded. "I felt it—going out of me. Sort of free. It'll be all right now. You needn't run away, Emma. God will attend to it. But of course sometimes He doesn't answer straight off. You have to go on asking."

"Why?"

"I don't know. Daddy says that if we got everything as soon as we asked, we wouldn't learn patience. And we would never learn to trust Him. And that's terribly important."

"Bother patience and trusting! There isn't *time*. Tell Him it's urgent."

"He knows that, Emma. But I'll remind Him if you like. And I'll go on asking. And it wouldn't be a bad idea if you asked too. He likes to make new friends."

"Well . . . but if He's going to keep me waiting until it's too late—what use will *that* be? I'm hungry, Lucy. I'm going home."

CHAPTER FIVE

THE PROMISE

WITH Emma gone the park felt lonely, and Lucy went home too. As she opened the gate she saw her father examining the old pear tree. "The fruit is going to be late this year, Lucy."

"Yes," she answered.

She loved the old tree; the blossom, the fruit, the gentle shade on hot summer days—the only shade there was in the garden. There used to be two, but three years ago one had died.

"Still, there's a fine crop."

"Yes," she answered.

She didn't feel, at that moment, that she could talk about anything, not even the pear tree. She felt too muddled and queer inside, too guilty.

"Your heels—are they better, my sweet?"

"Getting better."

"And how much money did you raise?"

Lucy gave a gasp of despair. She didn't know what to say. And there he was, his face full of interest, waiting . . .

"Quite a lot," she said.

"How much is a lot?"

"I've not—added it up." There, she'd done it again. That was another lie.

"Then let's add it together, shall we?"

Now what was she going to do?

He held out his hand. She slipped hers into it, and they went together into the house.

"Tea won't be long," he said, as they sat down. "Now, where's your card?"

"Here, Daddy."

"Now let me see . . . you walked eleven miles, and with four sponsors at five pence a mile and four at three pence—how much is that?"

"It's—three pounds, fifty-two new pence."

"Good. And my five pence a mile will make it four pounds, seven pence. Is that right?"

"Ye-es . . . oh . . . *Daddy*—thank you!"

Taking the money from him she wanted to run away fast and hide. Instead, she put her arms round him and kissed his cheek, as he expected her to do. And he caught her close, and held her, hugging her tight. In the middle of the hug Mrs. Ducker came in to say tea was ready.

"Colder weather next week," Mr. Winter said.

"Yes," said Lucy, her eyes on her plate.

"Lucy, are you quite well?"

"Yes, Daddy." She had seen the concern in his face and she hardly dared to look at him.

"Is there something on your mind, then?"

She hesitated, and then she said: "No, Daddy." And something in her mind began to scream at her— you're making it worse! You're lying *again*.

"What's making you so quiet, then?"

All she could do was shake her head.

"You're pale, my sweet. You're tired. You must go to bed early."

"Yes, Daddy."

She hated going to bed early. Her father knew it, and she saw the surprise on his face. If she could only chatter away as she usually did he would stop wondering what was the matter, but she couldn't. There was no bubble in her.

All she could think of was the longing to creep away by herself, to hide like a hedgehog, until that horrible guilty feeling went away.

It nagged at her. It was as hard to bear as a bad pain. It spoiled everything. Even the jigsaw puzzle her father had given her last week held no interest. She kept turning the pieces over and over and she couldn't make them fit. At last she said: "I'm tired, Daddy. I'll go to bed."

"Sleep tight, my sweet."

But the good-night kiss he gave her seemed all wrong. That guilty feeling made her father's face feel hard, like wood. By the time she got to her room, with its wide window looking out over the pear tree, she was almost in tears. Flinging herself down by the bed she cried: "Please, God—take it away . . ."

The rose-pink bedspread lay smooth on her bed, without a wrinkle. It didn't stuff the words back into her mouth. Perhaps it never had. It was only a bedspread. It wasn't alive. It didn't care how she prayed, right or wrong. It didn't know right from wrong.

But it *ought* to know! And she caught it up in her hands and shook it. It was the thing closest to her, the thing she buried her head in, trying to find out what she should do. She needed to know, and there was no one to tell her. No Mummy. She needed someone close to her. Someone to whom she could whisper all those things that worried her—her own mistakes, and Emma's. But she had promised Emma she wouldn't tell.

A bedspread wasn't any use! She hammered it with her fists. There was only God. And He was so big and great He made her feel afraid. He was close to her—oh yes . . . and yet He seemed so far away. Like a stranger. A great, powerful stranger who said: *What have you done?*

"Please, God," she cried, "I didn't mean it! I didn't mean it . . . forgive . . ."

It was lonely kneeling there, with God so far away, sitting on His Judgement Seat. She wanted Him to come down, and talk to her, as Jesus did with the fishermen. She wanted Him to come close. "Come near," she cried, "come near. Please God—come close to me."

She thought it was a silly prayer because she *knew* He was close. It was like feeling for someone in the dark, like Blind Man's Buff, flinging your arms about trying to touch the one you knew was there, somewhere. And although she thought it was silly she said it again.

"Please, God, come close to me."

And right then, she thought of Mrs. Robinson!

She saw herself, Lucy Winter, with money in her hand. She was giving it back to Mrs. Robinson, and Mrs. Robinson—she looked most surprised.

And then she saw herself with Mrs. *Murdock*!

And then——

"No!" she cried aloud. "I can't do *that*! I can't take the money *back*!

Why not?

"I *can't*!" she cried. "I—can't."

You're a liar and a thief.

She spun round. Who said *that*?

Emma, of course.
Bother Emma.

Slowly she crawled into bed, deep down, drawing the bedspread over her head. Lying there, the tears came back, to roll down her cheeks, wetting her pillow. She had asked God to come close, and He had . . . and she hated the thing He had asked her to do.

If she didn't give the money back, what then?

How *could* she give it back? If she did, everybody would know she was a thief, and a liar.

Emma knew already. Emma scorned her. Emma wouldn't do what she had done. Yet she *had* done it for Emma, or—partly for Emma. Which just went to show that it was no use doing wrong things to help people! To help people you had to do what was right.

Suppose her father found out?

That was what worried her as she lay in the darkness. Or at least, it was the biggest worry. The next biggest was how much money she was going to hand in for Oxfam. She had to take what she had collected to Mr. Craig tomorrow. Mr. Craig knew how far she'd walked, so what was she going to do with the rest of the money if she didn't give it back?

She could spend it, buy something for herself, get rid of it that way. Then her father would want to know where it had come from. And she would feel guilty all the time, afraid, wondering if she were going to be found out

She could put the money in the church collection, a bit at a time! *That* might get rid of her guilty feeling. But would God like stolen money? She was sure He wouldn't. If Emma didn't want to touch such stuff, you couldn't expect a righteous God to say thank you for it.

Oh, why had she done it? And what could she do now? Who could she ask? Not her father. He'd be far too upset. And cross. Not Mr. Craig. She was too ashamed. What would she say? What would he think of her?

Burrowing into her pillow, she longed to fall asleep. She curled in a ball, lay out straight. She wriggled, turned, tossed her head.

There was no one to ask, but the Lord Jesus Christ. And she knew what He would say! He'd told her to take the money back——

How *could* she? It was too *hard*. A good, kind Lord wouldn't ask her to do anything so hard.

But He had.

How *could* He ask her to do it? If she obeyed, everyone would know what a wicked girl she was, and she had always wanted people to think she was good.

She had thought so herself. She saw now that she wasn't good at all. What was the use of pretending to be what you weren't? Yet she wasn't pretending. She had really thought she was a good girl. Now she knew what she was. A thief. And a liar.

"Dear Lord Jesus—what shall I do?"

The words came out of her mouth loud—though she never meant them to. And she never heard her father's footsteps on the stairs. He didn't go into his room and shut the door as he usually did; he came into her room instead.

"Aren't you asleep, Lucy child?"

"No, Daddy, not yet." Hastily brushing tears away, she hoped he wouldn't switch on her light.

He didn't. He said, "When we're short of strength, Lucy, we can always rely on God for it."

"Yes, Daddy."

"You won't forget, my sweet?"

"No . . . I won't forget."

She had forgotten. She didn't want to remember. It was something she knew well, because her mother had told her time and again, but . . . how *could* she take that money back? She wanted to forget all about it, to make herself believe she had never done any such thing.

She turned over, thumped the pillow. She couldn't drive it out of her mind. "Please, God," she cried, "*go away!*" But she was careful not to say that out loud. She whispered it, in case her father heard. A prayer like that would shock him. He prayed that God would never leave him; but then, he was good, and she wasn't.

To know she wasn't good . . . that was a blow to Lucy's pride.

"Please, Lord Jesus—leave me alone."

Suppose He did?

Suppose He left her all alone in this wicked world? Suppose He took away her father and left her quite alone? What would she do? The thought made her panic. "No, no," she cried, "don't leave me alone. Don't! Don't!"

She was so upset she wondered if she'd cried out loud? Had her father heard? She listened, but all was quiet.

Slowly her heart beats eased. "Please, Lord Jesus, don't leave me alone. I'll do as you say, Lord. I will, if . . . You'll help me."

She sighed then, a sigh that shook her from head to foot. She had made a solemn promise and she would have to keep it. Lying there, she wondered how the Lord Jesus Christ gave you the strength to do the things you didn't want to, things that terrified you?

She'd learn, she supposed. She'd find out. "Help me, dear Lord."

And then she fell asleep.

She didn't know she'd fallen asleep, but the next moment it was morning! The blackbird was singing in the pear tree and the sun was streaming through the window. She could hear her father splashing in the bathroom. And there was a smell of bacon.

Her father didn't go to business on Saturdays. Today he would be out in the garden mowing the lawn. She would go to the park to meet Emma; they always met there on Saturdays. She couldn't invite Emma home because Mrs. Ducker didn't like her bringing children in the house. And Lucy never went to Emma's house because—well—Emma hadn't invited her. Emma's father was rich, and that made a difference. Emma said her mother was always entertaining.

"Sleep well, Lucy?" her father asked, as they sat down to breakfast.

"Yes, when I'd——"

Her father lifted his brows. "When you'd what, my sweet?"

Oh, *bother*! Why had she gone and said *that*! She

couldn't tell her father what happened last night. She saw he was waiting. And when her father had that waiting look you had to answer, and you had to tell the truth.

"When I'd . . . promised God."

He looked surprised. "What did you promise?"

Lucy picked up her spoon, and made a hole in her porridge. "Do I have to say?"

"Not if you don't want to."

"Well . . . it's a secret."

"Between you and the Lord?"

Lucy nodded. "Yes," she said. It was bad enough having to do what you'd promised without having to tell your father all about it! The thought appalled her. It took her appetite away.

When he offered her toast she shook her head. That made his eyebrows lift again. "It must have cost you something, Lucy—that promise?"

She nodded. She didn't want to talk about it. She was dreading what she had to do.

"Where are you going, Lucy, this lovely morning?"

"To the park," she said, "to meet Emma."

CHAPTER SIX

WHERE IS EMMA?

BUT when Lucy got to the park there was no sign of Emma.

Sitting on their usual seat, Lucy waited. Waited and waited. Where was Emma? She always came on Saturday mornings. What *could* she be doing?

The sun was shining, the birds were singing, the flowers were spreading their petals wide—but the day was all wrong. There was no Emma, and Lucy was miserable. She had that awful promise to keep all alone.

Still, now that she'd made it she felt better. She would keep it, and the Lord Jesus Christ would keep His. He had promised never to leave her. Lucy kept thinking of this as the time dragged by. But where was Emma?

Fear crept into Lucy's mind. She pushed it away. *That* couldn't be why Emma hadn't come. And she was going to jolly well tell her what she thought of her when she saw her! Oh, what was the use of sitting here? Opening her handbag, she counted out the coins. Mrs. Robinson—she'd do her first.

But what was she going to say?

And suppose Emma came, after all? Suppose she was just late? Something might have happened to prevent her coming. It must have done. She couldn't believe that Emma had . . . run away.

She was mean if she had! She should have waited.

Poor Mrs. Knight—what would she do? And poor Mr. Knight.

Lucy felt so sorry for them. Sorry for herself too. Everything was wrong. Lonely, forlorn, she wanted her mother. Someone to hold her in loving arms and comfort her. Someone to make lovely apple pies instead of those stodgy puddings Mrs. Ducker made. Someone to—but what was the use . . .

Bother! Bother! She ran from the park, and before she realised where she was she was there, in Merton Lane, at Mrs. Robinson's, flinging open the front gate—

She put her finger on the bell—quick, in case she took fright and ran away.

That had done it! She hoped wildly that Mrs. Robinson was out. But the door opened.

"Why, it's Lucy!"

Dropping her eyes, Lucy stared at her feet.

"Are you lonely, love?"

Lucy nodded. How would she ever begin? She sniffed, because the tears were stirring and she mustn't cry, and into her nostrils came——

"Oh," she exclaimed, "what a lovely smell!"

"Well now, in you come." Mrs. Robinson's arms were round her. "Now I wonder how you knew, Lucy, that I was baking apple pasties?"

"I didn't," cried Lucy. "I came because—oh, I told you a lie. I stole from you. I cheated you. I'm terribly sorry. I wish I'd never done it. I've come to bring the money back——"

"Well, I declare!"

Mrs. Robinson's mouth fell wide open. She looked

shocked. Dreadfully shocked. And puzzled. "How ever did you manage to do all that?"

"I didn't walk fifteen miles. Only eleven." And opening her handbag, Lucy took out the money and laid it on the table. Then she stood, waiting, looking down at her feet.

Mrs. Robinson didn't seem to know what to say. And Lucy didn't dare raise her eyes to look at her face. She could hear the clock ticking, and all of a sudden Mrs. Robinson said: "Well! I daresay those apple pasties are just about done! Could you eat one, my love?"

Lucy raised her eyes to find that Mrs. Robinson was smiling. Actually smiling. She heaved a little trembling sigh. What a relief!

"Oh . . ." she whispered, "*please*. Mummy used to make apple pies and apple pasties."

"Mine won't be as good as hers," Mrs. Robinson replied, going to the kitchen to take a baking sheet, full of pasties, brown, sizzling, and gloriously scented, out of the oven, "but they'll be the next best thing. There, my precious—mind now, it's hot. Better have this fork."

"Thank you," said Lucy, "oh, thank you!"

When she'd finished it and scraped the plate clean she gave Mrs. Robinson a great big hug, and asked if she could come again? Mrs. Robinson said she could. At the same time she thrust a parcel of pasties into Lucy's hands and said: "Take these, my love. And thank you for bringing that money back. That took courage, I'll be bound!"

Now for waspish Mrs. Murdock! It was well known that Mrs. Murdock wasn't always in the same good humour as Lucy had found her when last she called. Lucy wondered what her mood would be today. She soon found out, for the door flew open—

"*Now* what do you want? If you're coming here begging again for them Oxfam people it's just no good. It cost me enough last time!"

"Too much," said Lucy, looking at the ground.

"Too much? What are you saying?"

"I—made a mistake. I——"

"You made a *mistake*! What did you do?"

"I—didn't walk fifteen miles as I said, it was only eleven."

"You wicked girl!"

"Yes," said Lucy.

"Telling lies. Cheating me. Well, I declare! What have you done with the money then? Brought it back? You *wicked* girl."

"Yes," said Lucy.

"Umm," said Mrs. Murdock. "So you know you're wicked?"

"Yes," said Lucy, hanging her head.

"Well, you're better than a lot. There's plenty don't know." She fingered the coins. "What made you bring this money back?"

Lucy hesitated. "God made me."

"*God*," said Mrs. Murdock. And the astonishment that flashed across her face had Lucy near to laughter. "So *that's* how it is! You and Him is friends like?"

"Yes," said Lucy, for she was beginning to feel that that was true.

"Him and me is friends too. And if He can be friends with a queer old stick like myself, He'll do wonders for you, girl. Here, Lucy Winter, buy yourself some chocolate."

"Oh . . ." said Lucy, not wanting to take the money, for Mrs. Murdock's cardigan had a hole in the elbow. "Can you spare it?"

"Of course I can spare it. I'm an old growler." Mrs. Murdock's mood changed all of a sudden, and she patted Lucy's shoulder as she had done the last time, saying: "It's a fine girl you're getting." She pressed the money into Lucy's hand and said: "There! Take it."

"Thank you," said Lucy, "you're terribly kind."

That afternoon she had to take the money for Oxfam to Mr. Craig at the end of the avenue. Dinner over, Lucy helped Mrs. Ducker to wash up, wiping the dishes. Then off she ran.

She said, as soon as she was through the door, "Mr. Craig, has Emma been?"

"Emma?" He looked blank.

"You know, my friend Emma Knight. Don't you remember?" Emma, so tall and fair. How could anyone forget Emma?

"Oh yes," he said, "I remember now. The girl with the long legs. She brought her money yesterday. Last night."

"*Last night?*" Lucy stood staring. "But it's this afternoon we have to bring it."

"Yes, I know, but she explained that she couldn't come this afternoon."

"Couldn't *come*?" said Lucy, and she didn't know what to think. But as she watched him count her money she saw how long his fingers were, and when he thanked her with a smile she thought it almost worth the blisters. But where could Emma be? She walked home deep in thought.

Perhaps Emma had gone to the park this afternoon instead of this morning. Off Lucy rushed—but there was no Emma sitting on the seat. She still had to take back the rest of the money, but she was so worried about Emma it crowded everything else out of her mind. She had to know where Emma was.

And there was only one way to find out.

It was less than five minutes walk to Maple Road and Lucy ran. She was looking in through the gates of Emma's home in two minutes flat. No sign of Emma. She wasn't lying in the sun as Lucy thought she might be.

The house was lovely. Not old and romantic like Bessley Manor, but a wonderful place to live.

It had been her secret dream for months that Emma would say: Come to my house to play; but Emma never had.

Tall trees, smooth lawns. When she grew up she was going to live in a house like this, with a garden with trees like those—the monkey puzzles, the weeping willows. Because she could never hope to live in a house like Bessley Manor.

She couldn't really expect to live in a house like this either, but she was going to ask God to make it happen. But suppose that that was not a right prayer? She felt somehow that it wasn't. It might not be stuffed back into your mouth—it might not be as bad as that. Just labelled *Not Important* and put on one side to be considered later. Because you could be just as happy in a house like Pear Trees.

D

But she hadn't time to think about all that now. She had to walk up those steps and ring the doorbell and ask where Emma was. And the moment she rang, the door opened. A woman stood there. She must be Emma's mother. Lucy asked, trembling a little: "Is Emma in?"

"No, she isn't."

"Oh," said Lucy, biting her lip.

"What do you want?" asked Mrs. Knight. All that Emma had said about her was true. She was lovely to look at. "Who *are* you?" she said, and she sounded impatient, as though what she wanted was to get Lucy off the doorstep as fast as she could. But Lucy wasn't going yet.

"I'm Lucy," she said, "and Emma's my friend. I've brought her this," and she held out the chocolate she'd bought with Mrs. Murdock's money. "It's to make her feel better."

"But she isn't ill."

"No," said Lucy. "Just sad."

"Sad!" said Mrs. Knight. And Lucy knew she wasn't pleased. "Did you say *sad*?" Her face twisted and Lucy saw a tear roll down her cheek.

"Would you like my hanky?" Lucy asked, holding out the clean one she had in her pocket. She knew how uncomfortable it could be if you had no handkerchief at such a moment.

But poor Mrs. Knight didn't seem to mind about the tears rolling down. "Who *are* you?" she cried. "Do you know where Emma is?"

"No," said Lucy. "Don't you?"

"She didn't come home last night. We've informed the police."

"The police!" said Lucy, and all of a sudden she felt so weak she had to sit down on the step.

"You'd better come inside," said Mrs. Knight, "and tell me everything you know."

"I don't know anything," Lucy answered. But when Mrs. Knight held the door wide she got up from the step and went in, because she wondered what it was like inside.

It was full of flowers. And the chairs looked as though no one ever sat on them, which couldn't be true, for Mrs. Knight was sitting on one now, and so was she. It was a very comfortable chair too; you sank right down in it.

Lucy couldn't think how Emma had the courage to run away from a home like this. "She can't have gone far," she said, thinking aloud. "She hasn't much money."

"How do you know?" asked Mrs. Knight.

"Because——" Lucy stopped. There—she'd gone and said the wrong thing again! She had promised Emma she wouldn't tell, and she *wouldn't*. And yet she was sorry for Mrs. Knight. Her eyes were so anxious and she kept twisting her hands; she was very upset. "Well," said Lucy, "Emma said she didn't have much pocket money."

Mrs. Knight stiffened. "It's quite enough for a girl of eleven. She's never content."

"She's not happy, you see."

"She has everything to make her happy."

"Oh, no, she hasn't!"

"She *hasn't*?"

"No . . . you see . . . she wants you and—you and her Dad—to be happy together. To . . . love one another. That would make her terribly happy."

"But——" Mrs. Knight's face turned red. "We *are* happy together. We *do* love one another."

"Oh . . . Emma must have been mistaken."

"Lucy, what did Emma say to you? What did she tell you? Lucy—did Emma hear? Tell me. You *must* tell me. Lucy, it's important."

Lucy looked down at her shoes. She felt Mrs. Knight ought to know why Emma had run away, and she hadn't promised not to tell that——

"She heard you quarrelling," she said, her voice a whisper. "She heard you say you'd send her away to boarding school, and she was—afraid that—when she came back there'd be no home. She was going to run away because——"

"Because *what*?" Mrs. Knight was pulling at her necklace.

"Because she thought you'd be upset and you'd miss her so much you'd make it up. You wouldn't quarrel any more. I mean"—Lucy's voice rose to a shout—"if Emma's run away it's because she wants you to love her Dad."

"But I do love her Dad!"

"Oh," said Lucy in a crestfallen voice. "And does her Dad love you?"

"Of course he does! And I really think you are a very impudent little girl."

"Oh . . . I didn't mean to be. Really I didn't. I'm not rude really. I'm worried about Emma, and Emma's worried about you——"

"Emma's only a little girl and she doesn't know what it is to be—well—to be——"

"She knows what it is to be Emma!" and Lucy bounced up from the chair. "I must go now." She was beginning to understand why Emma had run away. The house didn't feel right. There was no comfy togetherness, no *safe* feeling. And Mrs. Knight—she was all wrong too. She made Lucy think of a piece of elastic stretched out tight.

Ping! Ready to snap back fast and upset everything! That was what was worrying Emma. Lucy wondered if Emma's Dad was like that too?

"I must go now," Lucy said again, although she was almost out of the door. How queer, that such a lovely house could make you feel so very unhappy. She was glad to be running past the lawns, past the gently swaying trees, out of the gate. She was glad to be going home.

CHAPTER SEVEN

SHAME

REACHING the avenue, Lucy slackened her steps. What now? If only she knew where Emma was. She stopped to peer over the wall into Mr. Craig's garden. It was bright with roses and other flowers, and he'd made a rock garden at the side of the house, by the greenhouses where the orchids were, and the orange tree. It was newly planted with pansies, rock roses, polyanthus, pinks and bellflowers, and dozens of plants she couldn't name.

She turned away. She wanted to paint trees. She always wanted to paint trees when she felt like this. But she was tired of the trees in the park. She'd drawn those too often. She longed for great trees gnarled with age, or growing straight and tall, like those at Bessley Manor. At the thought of where her longings led her she drew in her breath, sharp. She couldn't go there, not to the manor!

There were cedars of Lebanon in the manor grounds, and a mulberry tree. Or so her father said. She had never seen a mulberry tree. But you could see the cedars from the road, and it was those she longed to paint. Cedars of Lebanon. She loved the name. It made her think of a babbling brook.

There were weeping willows and silver firs. Aspens, birches, and walnut trees—all at Bessley Manor. The thought of them made her longing grow.

Her father was still busy hoeing when she rushed home—up the avenue, in through the gate. Hearing the gate click, he turned round and said, "Lucy, where have you been?"

"Daddy—Emma's run away."

He looked at her as though she was talking nonsense. "I asked you, Lucy—where have you been?"

"To Emma's house. Daddy, she's gone! She said she would and oh, I'm so worried."

"Are you, Lucy? So am I. Is what I've heard *true*?"

She noticed then that he was frowning. She saw the anger in his eyes. She thought, he *knows*! Oh, what shall I do? He's found out that I'm a thief and a liar. Somebody's told him.

"Is it true, Lucy—what I've heard?"

"You mean——" Lucy dropped her eyes. She couldn't stand that angry gaze. "You mean about the money?"

"Yes, Lucy. *You*, my child, my daughter—how could you do such a thing?"

"*Daddy*——"

"I'm ashamed of you, Lucy."

"Oh, *Daddy* . . ." she flung herself into his arms, "*please* . . . please listen. I——"

He held her from him, and she had never seen his face so stern. Oh, what could she say?

"Daddy——" she buried her face in the crook of his arm, "don't look at me like that."

"How do you expect me to look at you, Lucy? And I am still waiting for an explanation."

"I wanted the money for Emma," she whispered, "so she could run away. But she wouldn't take it. She's gone without. And——"

"Yes, Lucy. What else?"

"I didn't want to say I'd walked only eleven miles. Emma walked twenty."

"Emma has not been ill."

"And she doesn't get blisters. Oh, Daddy, I'm sorry. I wish I'd never done it. But I'm taking the money back. I've taken Mrs. Robinson's and Mrs. Murdock's and—Daddy—do you remember last night when you came up to bed, you said God always gives us strength, and Daddy—He has. I didn't think I *could* take that money back—I didn't think I could *possibly* do it, I was so ashamed of what I'd done—but—I *am* doing it! It's just that I'm . . . worried about Emma," and she lifted her face from her father's sleeve and looked up at him.

That awful, angry look was gone. His face was all gentle. But she couldn't be sure what he was thinking. He looked perplexed, as though he didn't know what to think.

"Lucy, I don't know what to say to you."

"Why, Daddy?"

"You're such a mixture of good and bad."

"But I thought everybody was!"

"Well, yes, they are. But I want you to be more good than bad. A lot more good. Lucy, did you encourage Emma to run away?"

"Of course I didn't! I told her it was wicked."

"But Lucy, you've just told me that you told that lie and took that money because you wanted it for Emma."

"I know, but—Daddy, I *did* try to stop her. I prayed—and if she'd waited God *would* have answered my prayer. He would, Daddy, wouldn't He? He would have made everything come right?"

"Yes, Lucy, but—you must remember, child, that God doesn't always answer our prayers in the way we expect. His ways are not our ways, you know. His ways are much higher." And Lucy felt that he was blaming *her* for what Emma had done! He believed she had encouraged Emma. And . . . it looked as though she had. She had stolen the money so Emma could run away.

Yet that wasn't all the truth. But she couldn't explain. And there was no one to help her.

The police came that night.

Lucy was standing at the bedroom window when she saw the police car. She watched in horror as it stopped. She watched the policemen climbing out. Together they opened the gate and walked to the door.

Her heart was beating so hard in her throat she felt it would jump right out of her mouth. What would her father say when he opened the door to find two policemen on the step? They had come about Emma, of course.

"Lucy! Lucy!" She could hear the concern in her father's voice. "Lucy, the police are here!"

They were all standing in the hall. As her foot touched the last stair, the older one said: "Well now, Lucy—you know a girl called Emma Knight?"

Lucy nodded. "Yes," she whispered.

"And you knew she meant to run away?"

"No—I mean—I didn't think she would."

"You didn't *think* she would. Why?"

"Because . . . I thought she'd wait——"

"Wait? What for?"

"She should have waited," Lucy said. "She should have given God time. You see, we asked Him to help and I thought she'd wait, but . . . she couldn't have done——"

The policeman laid a hand upon her shoulder. "What did you need to be praying about?"

"About Emma's Mum and Dad. They aren't happy, you see. And she thought——"

"Yes—what did she think?"

"She thought they'd be upset—terribly upset— and that would bring it right again."

A smile hovered round the policeman's mouth. "You mean, Lucy, that Emma Knight has run away to give her parents a right good scare?"

"Yes," said Lucy. "Yes, that's it."

"And you know where she's gone?"

"No. No, I don't. She wouldn't tell me." She grasped the policeman by the arm. "Please—please find her."

The policeman nodded. "We'll try, Lucy. Yes, we'll find her." And they said good night to her father and tramped out of the house.

CHAPTER EIGHT

TRESPASSING

Lucy couldn't sleep that night. She wondered if Emma was asleep. Was she hungry and thirsty and cold? Shivering in some old barn?

The hours of the following day dragged by. One o'clock . . . two . . . three . . . four . . . When the clock struck four, Lucy could resist the urge no longer. She must go—she must go! She threw paper, brushes, paints, into her school case. Dashed out through the door—through the gate, letting it bang—down the avenue—running—running——

She felt driven, like the dust the breeze was whirling. She would have to catch a bus, and the fare would be a lot. It would be worth it, though, to get to Bessley Manor. She couldn't walk, not all that way. Her heels were still sore.

As she ran to the stop a bus drew up, and she was lucky! It was a 290, the right one. She hopped on board. And as she sat there, silently, the trees began to call again. Come . . . come . . . come . . . they whispered, the cedars of Lebanon, the great frothy limes, the spruce, the larch, the beech, and the oak. Come, come, come, they called. In her rising excitement Lucy clasped her hands tight. All else slipped from her mind. She was going to Bessley Manor—at long last. And alone.

They were nearly there! Clatter, clatter, down the stairs—to jump off as the bus stopped. She began to run. The house was waiting for her. It had been waiting for years for her to skip along its drive, touching the trees with her fingers.

Close now to the old grey walls, she wondered what tales the house would tell her? It was so old that all its tales might be long forgotten. It might be asleep. It might have been sleeping for years, since the day the old squire died.

Skipping out on to what had once been a lawn, Lucy looked up. Her gaze travelling from window to window she cried aloud, "I love you," and flung her arms wide. She listened, but there was no reply, only the rustle of the wind in the trees.

What did you do when you had no key and all the doors were locked and bolted? Trespassers, the notice said, would be prosecuted. Still, if by chance she found a door that stood wide open she could go right in, and that would not be trespassing.

That she was trespassing already never once occurred to Lucy. Gazing up at all the windows, thinking her delighted thoughts, she didn't see the man by the side door, watching her.

Yet she might have done if something hadn't caught her eye. For something moved. Behind one of those windows someone waved. It couldn't be? No, it couldn't, but staring up——

Her heart gave a great bound! It was Emma. *Emma.* Of course! Why hadn't she thought of it before? She should have known that this was where Emma would come. But how had she got in? Lucy was just about to wave back, to let Emma know she'd seen her, when she saw the man.

What was *he* doing here?

Spoiling it all! And then she saw who he was.

It was Mr. Craig.

He had taken a key from his pocket and was open-ing the side door. Just as though he owned the place! Should she hide behind the holly hedge or——

She couldn't hide from Mr. Craig. So she ran right up to him and said, "Hello!"

She expected him to smile at her, that his eyes would twinkle as they had before. But he didn't seem the same today. "You're trespassing," he said. "You've no right here."

"I came to paint the trees," she said.

"You saw the sign. You've no right here. I've been watching you. You're trying to break in."

"I'm not," said Lucy. "Really I'm not."

"Then get off home."

She bit her lip. He didn't seem the same at all. "Have you ever been inside?" she asked.

"Of course I've been inside."

"Oh . . ." said Lucy, with a long sigh.

"You silly child. I'm the agent for this estate. It's in my care. On my books. Has been for some time now." He gave a sudden smile. "Do you want to look round?"

"Oh, yes," cried Lucy in delight, "*please*." Then she remembered. Emma was in the house. He'd find her. "No," she said, and shook her head.

"You're not afraid—— ?"

"Of course I'm not afraid. But I'd rather not——"

"Then you'd better get off home," and Mr. Craig stepped inside, and banged the door shut.

He'd find Emma!

And she'd be trespassing. She'd be prosecuted.

Lucy hammered on the door and yelled, "Mr. Craig! Mr. Craig!"

The door was opened straight away. "Well?"

"I'd like to see the house," she said.

"So you changed your mind?"

"Yes, please. It would be very kind of you to show me round," and as she stepped inside she said, "I've been wanting to see inside this house ever since I was born."

"Really!" Mr. Craig's eyebrows lifted.

"Yes, really. I mean——"

Mr. Craig nodded, gravely. And though they weren't laughing as they usually did, his eyes were kind. "I know what you mean."

She said, in a loud voice so that Emma could hear, "Do you know that Emma's lost?"

They were going up the stairs. It was a wonderful staircase, wide and sweeping, and Lucy wanted to go up slowly, with time to stand and look about, but Mr. Craig seemed in a hurry. "Yes," he said, "I know she's lost. That's why I'm here."

"You mean," said Lucy as loud as she could, "you're *looking* for her?"

"That's what I mean."

"Oh . . ." said Lucy, wondering why he should be taking such an interest in Emma. Thinking of Mrs. Knight she said: "Her Mum's most awfully upset."

"Yes, very."

"Do you know her?" she asked, surprised.

"Of course," he answered.

"But you didn't know Emma the other day?"

He looked quite cross. "Perhaps I didn't. But

I do now. And you and I have got to find her." He began going up the stairs two at a time.

"Wait," cried Lucy, "wait! You're going too fast. You promised to show me round."

"I've got to find Emma. Her mother thought she might be here. She said Emma likes this house—talks about it. Silly girl, going off because——"

"Because what?" Lucy asked. "Do you *know* why she ran away?"

"Of course I know! Her mother told me." He sounded so impatient that Lucy said: "Wouldn't *you* feel just like Emma if *your* father and mother—well——"

"I wouldn't run away," said Mr. Craig sharply. "I'd accept it."

"Emma isn't going to. And she won't need to. Her father and mother do love each other, really. Mrs. Knight said they did. It's just some *man* that's got in the way. I wish," said Lucy, "I knew who it was. I'd tell him what I thought of him!"

He turned to face her. "And what *do* you think?"

"I think he's downright mean! I think he's *awful*. I think he's a sneak, and——"

"You can't find words that are bad enough, can you?"

"I can," she said. "I can find them all right, but I won't say them."

They had reached the attics. Lucy wondered where Emma could be? She didn't want Mr. Craig to find Emma. He was such a nice man really; she like him tremendously, and yet——

Suddenly he swung round and said in a vexed sort

of voice: "What *brought* you here? You didn't come here to paint trees. You can't expect me to believe that. You know where Emma is."

"I don't. And I *did* come here to paint trees. Look——" Lucy tossed out her brushes and pencils all over the floor. "I always paint when I'm miserable. It's that man's fault. He's making us all unhappy. He's plain bad—and I hate him."

"Oh, come now—give the poor man a chance. I'm sure he'll make Emma's mother very happy."

"How *can* you be sure?" Lucy stood, staring at him. "You're wrong," she said. "He won't make her happy. He *can't*. She loves Mr. Knight. She told me she did."

"She told you nothing of the sort."

"She did. She told me yesterday."

Mr. Craig stood then, smoothing his hair, for somehow or other it had got all tousled, and he looked sort of queer. Angry. Then round he went, opening doors, slamming them shut. There was no Emma, and no place where Emma could hide. Shrugging his shoulders, he set off down the stairs.

"I wish," said Lucy, following him, and gazing about her, "I lived in a house like this."

He didn't answer. "Emma!" he shouted, reaching the landing, "Emma, where are you?" Flinging open door after door, hardly waiting to look inside— "Emma!" he bellowed, "Emma—where are you? Your mother's upset."

No answer.

Down they went to the ground floor. Lucy, by this time, was quite sure she must have been mistaken. The house felt so cold. Sad, too, as though it sighed all day and all night. And how could Emma get in? Where could she hide?

Mr. Craig seemed upset, as upset as Mrs. Knight herself, and Lucy wondered why. He began to get bothered, Lucy thought, when I said that Emma's Mum *did* love Emma's Dad.

Mr. Craig said sharply, "Come along, I'm going now. I'm locking up."

"But I haven't seen the house," said Lucy.

"Of course you've seen it."

"Not as I meant," said Lucy with a sigh. "I wanted to pretend I lived here. So you won't mind, will you, if I stay and paint?"

"Paint what?"

"The trees. I *told* you."

"I don't think——"

"*Please* let me stay." Lucy looked up with pleading eyes. He was going to refuse. "I won't harm the tiniest leaf. I promise I won't."

"No, I can't let you." Then a thoughtful expression stole over his face. "All right," he said. "But only for a short time."

Something had made him change his mind! "Thank you. Oh, thank you," she exclaimed, and she watched as he climbed in his car, and when she had waved him away it felt lonely. More lonely than she would admit. The trees were throwing long shadows across the grass. And they whispered, wearily.

CHAPTER NINE

THE GOOSE

LUCY shivered in the thin air. She wished now she'd gone home with Mr. Craig. But she had to know if Emma was in the house, or if she'd imagined it. And first of all she had to make sure that Mr. Craig had really gone.

That meant running all down the drive and back. Satisfied that she was alone, she walked round the house, looking up at every window.

No sign of Emma now. There was no one here but herself and the birds.

"Emma!" she shouted, "Emma!" Running round to the front door she hammered upon it.

She saw the bell then, the old-fashioned kind you pulled. She tugged hard—and the tingling and the clanging, she had never heard anything like it! As the noise died away she heard . . . *laughter*.

Right up the scale the laughter went. Ending with a little shriek.

Emma! Nobody else could laugh like that.

"Emma!" she shouted. "Open the door!"

Emma did. Sliding the bolts, she peered out.

"Has he gone?" she asked.

She didn't look a bit like Emma. Her face was pinched, dirty. Her eyes swollen and red from crying. Her lovely hair all tangled and wild.

"Oh, *Emma*—why did you do it?"

"Has he gone?" asked Emma again, her gaze sweeping the grounds. "Are you sure he's gone?"

"Yes, he's gone. Oh, Emma, why did you *do* it? Why didn't you wait?"

Emma's face changed. "I didn't do it for fun," she said. "It's not been fun."

"No," said Lucy. She could see it hadn't. "But, Emma, where did you hide?"

"In a cupboard, you goose."

"*I'm* not the goose," returned Lucy briskly. "*I* wasn't looking!"

Emma smiled, and the smile made her weary little face look better. "Come upstairs," she said. "Oh, Lucy, was I scared that man would find me! My heart beating—it made such a noise. But I could hear what you said—upstairs or down—or most of it. I've been so afraid. The nights! Here in this great big house, all alone. I've been frightened to death."

"But you're not dead," said Lucy.

"I'm sure I would have been, but for your God."

"But for my *God*?"

Emma sat down on the stairs. "I'm glad you told me about Him, Lucy. And about the Lord Jesus Christ. Because—well—it wasn't so bad when it was daylight—but when it got dark—Oh, *Lucy*, I was scared stiff. And—I talked to Him, Lucy. I talked to the Lord Jesus Christ. You say He's alive, and helps people, and I believe He does. Because when I'd talked to Him I felt better. Not nearly so frightened. And I crept upstairs to where it was moonlight. The shine came in on the floors. I curled up and fell fast asleep, though I was shivering cold. And when I woke up it was daylight again. I'm terribly hungry. Could you bring me some more food?"

"But Emma, aren't you coming home?"

"Not till I'm found."

"But you *are* found! *I've* found you."

"Oh, you don't count. That man—that goose——"

"It's Mr. Craig. He's the *agent*."

"He's not much good. There's a window without a catch. I pushed it up and crawled inside." Emma giggled. "But why was he looking for *me*? Does everyone know I'm lost?"

"The police are looking for you, Emma."

"Oh . . ." said Emma, her eyes wide. "Are they upset, Lucy? Mummy? Daddy?"

"Of course they're upset!"

"Are they?" Emma's mouth curved in delight. "How do you know?"

"I went to your house. I was so worried. Your mother—Emma, she was quite distracted."

"Distracted? Was she really?" Emma grinned. "That's good. That's what I meant. I wonder what made Mr.—what's his name—the goose, Mr. Goose —what made him get so cross?"

"I think," said Lucy, "it was what I said about your Mum loving your Dad. He didn't like it, Emma. Emma . . . you don't think . . . it couldn't be Mr. *Craig*, could it?"

"Mr. *Craig*?" Emma's mouth fell wide open.

Lucy bit her lip. She hadn't meant to say that. She liked Mr. Craig. Even when he was cross. She couldn't believe that he would——

"Mr. *Craig*?" Emma said. "Oh, Lucy, I wish I knew! I had to run away, you know."

"Why?"

"I had to show Mummy how much it *mattered*.

That day when I got home I heard them talking.
Mummy and the man. I listened at the door.
Mummy was saying she couldn't leave me, and he
was saying that I'd be all right. That I'd soon get
over it. But I *wouldn't*, Lucy. And what would
Daddy do?"

"Find someone else, I suppose," said Lucy.

"He wouldn't. He would *never* find anyone to love
like Mummy. I know, I can feel it here——" and
Emma laid both hands upon her chest. "So I
had to give them a fright. What else could I do? And
then there's the boys. Boys need a mother.
Mummy's always saying so, but—she must have
forgotten. What else could I do—except run away
before she did?"

When Emma argued it out like that all she said
made sound common sense, and Lucy hadn't a word
to say. After all, you couldn't expect Emma to do
nothing. Just wait for her world to crash about her.
She wasn't that sort of girl.

"Emma . . . what did the man's voice sound like?
Did it sound like Mr. Craig's?"

Emma frowned. "I can't be sure. But . . . I think
it did. His voice . . . gone all silky soft," and her
eyes grew wide as she thought of it.

Lucy, too, was lost in thought. Neither heard the
approaching car that pulled up well out of sight of
the house. Nor did they hear the soft swish-swish of
footsteps on the grass. Nor did they see the man
framed in the open doorway, until he said: "So you
you were here all the time!"

CHAPTER TEN

"LOOK WHAT THE WIND IS DOING!"

EMMA let out her breath in a soft whistle. Looking at Lucy with round eyes, she said: "It's the *goose*!" And up she got and walked down the stairs. "You've found me," she said.

"Yes, I've found you. And I'm going to take you both home—right away."

"You're a *goose*," said Emma, her voice hot with scorn, "to think Mummy could love *you* better than she loves Daddy," and she seemed to grow inches taller. "You don't know my father. He's marvellous. But *you*—you're a goose."

Mr. Craig flushed and stepped backwards. He didn't seem to know what to say. He looked angry, uncertain, as though he was wondering if he really *was* a goose? Emma had spoken with such confidence.

"Am I?" he said, as though talking to himself.

"Of course you are! You're—*ridiculous*. And," said Emma, "as well as a goose, you're a snake. A nasty, slippery, slimy snake. Ough!"

He turned and walked out of the house, to disappear among the trees.

"It's *him*!" cried Emma, her breast heaving. "I know it's him!"

Lucy didn't know what to say. She was astonished. And downcast, and sorry. That someone as nice as Mr. Craig could——

"I'm hungry!" said Emma. "I'm *starving*. I

want a potato pie. And pancakes. With chocolate sauce. And oh, Lucy, I'm tired. I'll have to go home now that I'm found. Oh, *bother*. I wonder where the old snake's gone?"

"To find out what he is, I suppose," said Lucy. "A goose or a snake. Yes, let's go home. Come on, bang the door! Emma, you're terribly dirty."

"What do I care? I'm *angry*, Lucy."

"Yes, I know. But your mother—what will she say? Emma, what will *you* say when you get home?"

"I haven't thought of that yet. I'm still thinking. I don't think I shall *say* anything. I think I shall go and wreck that man's greenhouse."

"Emma! It isn't right——"

"Why not?" cried Emma, her eyes blazing. "It's only a glasshouse. Why shouldn't I wreck it? He's stealing Mummy. He's wrecking my life!"

Lucy gave a gasp of despair. Battling with Emma was like battling with a high wind. She blew words all round you, she took your breath, she twisted your thoughts.

"Come on—come on—" Emma shrieked, "let's go, let's go!" And she was off—gone.

"Wait!" cried Lucy. She began to run. She must stop Emma. But she couldn't. Emma's legs were so much longer. Her feet were winged with indignation. She had no blisters on her heels. Still, thought Lucy, dashing down the long drive, Emma would have to wait for a bus. She'd catch up then.

But Lucy was wrong. At the bus-stop there was no Emma. She must have thumbed a lift. It was Sunday; there was not another bus for an hour.

Then Lucy remembered. She'd left her case, with her paints and brushes, locked up in the house.

There was time to go back. Mr. Craig would still be there. Among the trees where he'd taken refuge. He'd let her in.

She found him climbing into his car. She cried: "Please—I've left my paints in the house."

He climbed out then, and as they walked to the side door he took the key from his pocket. Lucy was wondering—should she tell him what Emma was threatening to do? Suddenly it occurred to her that in a fast car Emma could be there now.

"Hurry," she cried. "Oh, we must hurry——" and she dashed into the house to seize her things. "Hurry!" she shouted.

"Hurry? Why?"

"Your hothouses! Emma! She's going to smash them! Your hothouses!"

"My hothouses! My—but she can't!"

"She can," said Lucy. "And she will. She says you're stealing her mother—wrecking her life. So she's going to wreck your greenhouses!"

"Quick," he said, and broke into a run.

The car leapt forward. "She told you she was doing this? She *told* you?"

"Yes. I mean—she just thought of it—all of a sudden."

"You should know better! Children like you should know *better*. You're well brought up."

Lucy didn't answer for a while. She was busy, thinking. Then she said: "You love your greenhouses, Mr. Craig?"

"They're my greatest joy."

"Are they?" said Lucy, wonderingly. She had thought his greatest joy was Emma's mother. "They're only glass. You could build more."

"But my plants, you stupid girl. They'll *die*. You don't realize what I grow."

"I do. I've seen them over the wall. Orchids. And that orange tree. A banana plant grown all crooked. They're only plants." And to his astonishment—and his rage—she began to laugh.

"Stop that," he said, and drove faster. "You don't know what it would mean to me—to lose my houses! And to think that that girl——"

"You don't know what it would mean to Emma," Lucy cried, choking now with angry tears, "to lose her Mum!"

He slowed the car. "She won't lose her."

"Why?" cried Lucy, "why? Do you mean you've changed your mind?"

"Of course I haven't changed your mind."

"Oh . . ." said Lucy, her voice flat. A few more moments and she would know if Emma——"Please, God," she said, "don't let Emma smash the greenhouses."

"*What* did you say?"

Mr. Craig looked astonished. And Lucy, to her concern, suddenly realized she'd been praying aloud. She hadn't meant to. Glancing at Mr. Craig she wondered what on earth he'd think.

"I—I was asking God not to let Emma smash your greenhouse. I don't want her to, but I can't stop her, and . . ."

"You think God could?"

"Yes. I'm sure He could. Ask Him—quick. Before we turn the corner and see them—*smashed.*"

"She wouldn't dare——"

"Oh, she would. You don't know Emma when she's mad. And she's hopping mad. Oh . . . *look*——"

He slammed on his brakes and leapt from the car. They were just in time to see Emma, a stone from the rock garden in her hands. Then came the sound of shattering glass. Mr. Craig stood, dumb with dismay.

Lucy had leapt from the car by now. "Don't!" she screamed, "don't!" She rushed through the gate to catch Emma by the arm.

"No!" cried Emma, and she swung round—pushed her off. She wrenched another stone out of the earth, flung it—and laughed at the sound of the breaking glass. "There!" she said.

Smashed. Both hothouses with great gaping holes.

And Emma stood, watching, as the piercing wind, rushing in through the broken glass, tossed and broke the tender plants.

"They're cold," she said, looking at Mr. Craig, who stood there, silent.

"Yes," he said slowly. "They'll die."

Emma smiled. "Look, Mr. Goose—look what the wind is doing! *Look!*" Emma pointed as a sudden gust played havoc with the orchids' stems.

"You wretched child!"

In his anger he wrung his hands. And to Lucy's surprise he turned and left them. He went into the house and banged the door.

CHAPTER ELEVEN

A REAL MAN

As the door slammed behind him Lucy looked at Emma, and Emma at Lucy, and they sighed.

"Do you think," said Emma, "he's phoning the police?"

"Could be," said Lucy. "What will your father and mother say now?"

"Don't know," said Emma, kicking at a stone. "They'll send me away to school, I suppose. Out of control—that's what they'll say. And when I come back—*Lucy*—oh, *Lucy*—what shall I *do*?"

"Go home to your Mum," Lucy replied. "You've done enough!"

But to their surprise Emma's Mum came to them. The car swished round the corner and stopped—right in front of the goose's front door. They watched Mrs. Knight spring out. She didn't notice them, standing surrounded by broken glass. She didn't ring the bell, she rushed straight in. Emma went on kicking at the stone, and Lucy went on biting her lip. And the wind went on blowing—hustling and bustling, chilling and killing the tender plants.

"Do you think he phoned her?" Lucy asked, "to say we're here? Why else would she come?"

"To see *him*, stupid."

And then Emma's mother came out in a rage!

"Emma!" she shouted, "where have you been? And what have you done?" And she stared at the gaping holes, the wind-tossed plants.

Emma scowled. She did not answer.

"They'll die," groaned Mr. Craig. And he, too, stood and stared. "Oh, my orchids."

"They've lost their *mother*!" Emma shrieked, and her voice broke.

For a moment there was silence.

"She's right," cried Mrs. Knight, "she's right! They've got no mother. Warmth is their mother. They can't live without warmth. And water—that's their father. They need both to live. *Both*, Jeremy. They can't live without water. They can't live without warmth. They need both—father and mother. You know that—Jeremy?"

"Yes," he said, his voice tight. "I know."

"Then," she said, swinging round, facing him, "what are we going to do about *this* tender plant?" She pointed—to Emma.

"*She's* not a tender plant," he said.

"She is a tender plant." Emma's mother turned on her heel and walked away, back to the house. And Mr. Craig followed her.

"I *thought*," said Emma, "you said she was upset?"

"She is upset."

"She isn't glad to have me back," Emma cried. "She's in there with him and she doesn't care that I'm out here—" and she ripped up another stone to hurl at the greenhouse.

"Emma, stop! Stop!"

Emma gave a shout of laughter. Lucy flung herself upon her—tugged at the stone——

"Let go," she cried, "let go!"

But Emma held on—gave a tug—tore the stone out of Lucy's grasp—and fell—backwards.

On to the rock garden. On to a piece of glass. It had flown out to lodge there, standing on end. Emma, cut, her hand bleeding, saw the blood—drew a quick breath.

Then great gasping sobs shook Emma. "Emma!" Lucy screamed, and dashed indoors. "It's Emma!" she shrieked. "She's *killed*."

Silence. Then commotion. Mrs. Knight—Mr. Craig—flying out—And Lucy, frightened, exhausted, sank down on a chair.

How long she sat there she never knew. She heard the car drive away. Mr Goose came in.

"You naughty girl. You said she was killed."

"She was bleeding to death. I saw it—all that blood! It frightened me." Lucy, near to tears, looked up into his face.

Mr. Goose sat down. He looked just like her father had looked when her mother had died. Empty and crushed . . . like a broken egg. And Lucy wanted to lay her hand on his, but she didn't dare. She just waited. Suddenly he looked up. "It's no use," he said. "I can't stand it."

"Stand what?" cried Lucy. "Is Emma——?"

"Emma's all right. The cut's not deep. No . . . I cannot stand against such deep affection."

What was he talking about? Whose "deep affection"? He looked so sad. As though he'd lost something, something precious, something he loved. And then, the truth dawned.

"You mean—oh, Mr. *Goose*—you mean——"

"I shall move away. I'll keep an office in the town —that's all. Emma needn't worry any more. A tender plant can't stand a bitter wind."

A smile broke over Lucy's face. She had always thought he was a nice man, and now she knew he was. He was nice deep down. After all, everybody had temptations. She'd had hers. And he'd had his. And he'd won a great victory.

But he looked so sad. So defeated. She didn't know much about love yet, but she was quite sure it could almost tear you in two. It must be the hardest possible thing to say No to love, and when a man could say No because it was wrong—that called forth all her admiration. Mr. Goose was a man, a *real* man. Strong. He could fight a man's battle and gain a man's victory.

"He'll help you," she said, trying to comfort, "if you ask Him. He's helping me to take back the money I stole. He's good at giving strength."

"Who?" he exclaimed. "Who do you mean?"

"Oh—I thought everybody knew." Talking about God to a grown man made her feel shy. "Can't you guess?" she asked in a whisper.

"I suppose I can—as you're your father's daughter! He'll be wondering where you are?"

"Yes," she said, and got up. She felt lots better. "Do you think we could do it now?"

"Do what now?"

"Ask Him to help you. You'll need a lot of strength, you know. More than you've got."

"You're dead right," he exclaimed.

"Then—let's kneel down. He likes us to ask for things together."

He did not stir. He went on sitting with his head in his hands. And Lucy, kneeling, felt her face grow hot.

She knew God wanted to help Mr. Goose; to forgive him and to give him His strength. And if Mr. Goose didn't know how to ask she must help him. But she must be sure it was a right prayer, the sort Jesus would pray, so she began, "Our Father, which art in Heaven, Hallowed be thy Name. Thy Kingdom come. Thy will be done on earth, as it is in Heaven." She stopped; wondering what His will was.

What would God like Mr. Goose to do? And all at once she knew quite well what God would like, and with delight she rushed on.

"Please, God, help Mr. Craig to love you more than his plants or—anything else. Help him to make *You* his greatest joy. And give him lots of strength. And . . . forgive us our trespasses, as we forgive them that trespass against us—Mr. Goose—do you know what that means?"

"Yes," he said, "I know what it means. If Emma will forgive me, and I forgive Emma, God will forgive us both. And I do forgive Emma."

"Then He'll forgive you! And me too. Forgive us our trespasses, as we forgive them that trespass against us. For thine is the kingdom, the power, and the glory, for ever and ever, Amen.

"Are you happy now?" Lucy asked, jumping up.

"I shall be—one day, I suppose."

"Daddy'll think I'm lost—like Emma."

"It's getting dark. I'll see you home."

Early next morning Emma rang.

"Lucy," she said, "come to my house to play."

"Oh, Emma!"

"Yes. I'm going to tell you some wonderful news. Can you guess what?"

"No . . ." said Lucy, "I can't guess——"

"Mummy and Daddy! They hugged one another —then sat down and cried. *Cried*, Lucy. They're going to begin again! Isn't it wonderful?"

"Well," said Lucy, "I told you they would if you asked God to help."

"But, Lucy, doesn't He help in peculiar ways?"

"Well, you see—that was how it had to be. It was Mr. Goose! *He* needed help too. But he didn't ask. And can you guess what?"

"No," said Emma, "I couldn't guess what."

"Well—it's Mr. Goose. He's going to make God his greatest joy."

"Oh . . ." said Emma. "How'll he begin?"

"He's begun," said Lucy. "He's been forgiven!"

"Oh . . ." said Emma, "*that's* how you begin. You mean God forgave him. Is he going to consult Him when he gets in a fix?"

"Of course," said Lucy. "But we'll have to pray. He needs help badly. He's terribly sad."

"*Poor* Mr. Goose," Emma said briskly, "I know what I'll do! I'm going to forgive him. Then *I* can begin!"